Flower Fairies of the Autumn

AUTUMN

CICELY MARY BARKER

SEE ABOVE THE FAIRY'S
HEAD, GUELDER·ROSE'S
BERRIES RED.

THE BERRY-QUEEN

An elfin rout,
   With berries laden,
Throngs round about
   A merry maiden.

Red-gold her gown;
   Sun-tanned is she;
She wears a crown
   Of bryony.

The sweet Spring came,
   And lovely Summer:
Guess, then, her name—
   This latest-comer!

THE SONG OF
THE MOUNTAIN ASH FAIRY

They thought me, once, a magic tree
    Of wondrous lucky charm,
And at the door they planted me
    To keep the house from harm.

They have no fear of witchcraft now,
    Yet here am I today;
I've hung my berries from the bough,
    And merrily I say:

"Come, all you blackbirds, bring your wives,
    Your sons and daughters too;
The finest banquet of your lives
    Is here prepared for you."

(The Mountain Ash's other name is Rowan; and
it used to be called Witchentree and Witch-wood too.)

THE SONG OF
THE MICHAELMAS DAISY FAIRY

"Red Admiral, Red Admiral,
  I'm glad to see you here,
    Alighting on my daisies one by one!
I hope you like their flavour
  and although the Autumn's near,
    Are happy as you sit there in the sun?"

"I thank you very kindly, sir!
  Your daisies *are* so nice,
    So pretty and so plentiful are they;
The flavour of their honey, sir,
  it really does entice;
    I'd like to bring my brothers, if I may!"

"Friend butterfly, friend butterfly,
  go fetch them one and all!
    I'm waiting here to welcome every guest;
And tell them it is Michaelmas,
  and soon the leaves will fall,
    But *I* think Autumn sunshine is the best!"

THE SONG OF
THE WAYFARING TREE FAIRY

My shoots are tipped with buds as dusty-grey
As ancient pilgrims toiling on their way.

Like Thursday's child with far to go, I stand,
All ready for the road to Fairyland;

With hood, and bag, and shoes, my name to suit,
And in my hand my gorgeous-tinted fruit.

THE SONG OF
THE ROBIN'S PINCUSHION FAIRY

People come and look at me,
Asking who this rogue may be?
—Up to mischief, they suppose,
Perched upon the briar-rose.

I am nothing else at all
But a fuzzy-wuzzy ball,
Like a little bunch of flame;
I will tell you how I came:

First there came a naughty fly,
Pricked the rose, and made her cry;
Out I popped to see about it;
This is true, so do not doubt it!

THE SONG OF
THE ELDERBERRY FAIRY

Tread quietly:
O people, hush!
—For don't you see
A spotted thrush,
One thrush or two,
Or even three,
In every laden elder-tree?

They pull and lug,
They flap and push,
They peck and tug
To strip the bush;
They have forsaken
Snail and slug;
Unseen I watch them, safe and snug!

(These berries do us no harm, though they don't
taste very nice. Country people make wine from
them; and boys make whistles from elder stems.)

THE SONG OF
THE ACORN FAIRY

To English folk the mighty oak
   Is England's noblest tree;
Its hard-grained wood is strong and good
   As English hearts can be.
And would you know how oak-trees grow,
   The secret may be told:
You do but need to plant for seed
   One acorn in the mould;
For even so, long years ago,
   Were born the oaks of old.

THE SONG OF
THE DOGWOOD FAIRY

I was a warrior,
    When, long ago,
Arrows of Dogwood
    Flew from the bow.
Passers-by, nowadays,
    Go up and down,
Not one remembering
    My old renown.

Yet when the Autumn sun
    Colours the trees,
Should you come seeking me,
    Know me by these:
Bronze leaves and crimson leaves,
    Soon to be shed;
Dark little berries,
    On stalks turning red.

(Cornel is another name for Dogwood; and Dogwood
has nothing to do with dogs. It used to be Dag-wood, or
Dagger-wood, which, with another name, Prickwood,
show that it was used to make sharp-pointed things.)

THE SONG OF
THE BLACK BRYONY FAIRY

Bright and wild and beautiful
For the Autumn festival,
I will hang from tree to tree
Wreaths and ropes of Bryony,
To the glory and the praise
Of the sweet September days.

(There is nothing black to be seen about this Bryony,
but people do say it has a black root; and this may
be true, but you would need to dig it up to find out.
It used to be thought a cure for freckles.)

THE SONG OF
THE HORSE CHESTNUT FAIRY

My conkers, they are shiny things,
  And things of mighty joy,
And they are like the wealth of kings
  To every little boy;
I see the upturned face of each
  Who stands around the tree:
He sees his treasure out of reach,
  But does not notice *me*.

For love of conkers bright and brown,
  He pelts the tree all day;
With stones and sticks he knocks them down,
  And thinks it jolly play.
But sometimes I, the elf, am hit
  Until I'm black and blue;
O laddies, only wait a bit,
  I'll shake them down to you!

THE SONG OF
THE BLACKBERRY FAIRY

My berries cluster black and thick
For rich and poor alike to pick.

I'll tear your dress, and cling, and tease,
And scratch your hands and arms and knees.

I'll stain your fingers and your face,
And then I'll laugh at your disgrace.

But when the bramble-jelly's made,
You'll find your trouble well repaid.

THE SONG OF
THE NIGHTSHADE BERRY FAIRY

"You see my berries, how they gleam and
    glow,
Clear ruby-red, and green, and orange-
    yellow;
Do they not tempt you, fairies, dangling so?"
    The fairies shake their heads and answer "No!
    You are a crafty fellow!"

"What, won't you try them? There is
    naught to pay!
Why should you think my berries poisoned
    things?
You fairies may look scared and fly away—
The children will believe me when I say
    My fruit is fruit for kings!"
    But all good fairies cry in anxious haste,
    "O children, do not taste!"

(You must believe the good fairies, though the berries
look nice. This is the Woody Nightshade, which has
purple and yellow flowers in the summer.)

THE SONG OF
THE ROSE HIP FAIRY

Cool dewy morning,
    Blue sky at noon,
White mist at evening,
    And large yellow moon;

Blackberries juicy
    For staining of lips;
And scarlet, O scarlet
    The Wild Rose Hips!

Gay as a gipsy
    All Autumn long,
Here on the hedge-top
    This is my song.

THE SONG OF
THE CRAB-APPLE FAIRY

Crab-apples, Crab-apples, out in the wood,
Little and bitter, yet little and good!
The apples in orchards, so rosy and fine,
Are children of wild little apples like mine.

The branches are laden, and droop to the
            ground;
The fairy-fruit falls in a circle around;
Now all you good children, come gather
            them up:
They'll make you sweet jelly to spread
            when you sup.

One little apple I'll catch for myself;
I'll stew it, and strain it, to store on a shelf
In four or five acorn-cups, locked with a key
In a cupboard of mine at the root of the tree.

THE SONG OF
THE HAZEL-NUT FAIRY

Slowly, slowly, growing
　　While I watched them well,
See, my nuts have ripened;
　　Now I've news to tell.
I will tell the Squirrel,
　　"Here's a store for you;
But, kind Sir, remember
　　The Nuthatch likes them too."

I will tell the Nuthatch,
　　"Now, Sir, you may come;
Choose your nuts and crack them,
　　But leave the children some."
I will tell the children,
　　"You may take your share;
Come and fill your pockets,
　　But leave a few to spare."

THE SONG OF
THE WHITE BRYONY FAIRY

Have you seen at Autumn-time
Fairy-folk adorning
All the hedge with necklaces,
Early in the morning?
Green beads and red beads
Threaded on a vine:
Is there any handiwork
Prettier than mine?

(This Bryony has other names—White Vine, Wild
Vine, and Red-berried Bryony. It has tendrils to
climb with, which Black Bryony has not, and its
leaves and berries are quite different. They say its
root is white, as the other's is black.)

THE SONG OF
THE BEECHNUT FAIRY

O the great and happy Beech,
   Glorious and tall!
Changing with the changing months,
   Lovely in them all:

Lovely in the leafless time,
   Lovelier in green;
Loveliest with golden leaves
   And the sky between,

When the nuts are falling fast,
   Thrown by little me—
Tiny things to patter down
   From a forest tree!

(You may eat these.)

THE SONG OF
THE HAWTHORN FAIRY

These thorny branches bore the May
    So many months ago,
That when the scattered petals lay
    Like drifts of fallen snow,
     "This is the story's end," you said;
    But O, not half was told!
For see, my haws are here instead,
And hungry birdies shall be fed
    On these when days are cold.

THE SONG OF
THE PRIVET FAIRY

Here in the wayside hedge I stand,
And look across the open land;
Rejoicing thus, unclipped and free,
I think how you must envy me,
O garden Privet, prim and neat,
With tidy gravel at your feet!

(In early summer the Privet has spikes of
very strongly-scented white flowers.)

THE SONG OF
THE SLOE FAIRY

When Blackthorn blossoms leap to sight,
They deck the hedge with starry light,
    In early Spring
    When rough winds blow,
    Each promising
    A purple sloe.

And now is Autumn here, and lo,
The Blackthorn bears the purple sloe!
    But ah, how much
    Too sharp these plums,
    Until the touch
    Of Winter comes!

(The sloe is a wild plum. One bite will set your
teeth on edge until it has been mellowed by frost;
but it is not poisonous.)

FREDERICK WARNE

Published by the Penguin Group
Registered office: 80 Strand, London, WC2R ORL
Penguin Young Readers Group, 345 Hudson Street, New York, N.Y. 10014, USA

First published 1926
First published by Frederick Warne 1990
This edition first published 2008

Manufactured in China

Noah's Ark

Stories re-told by Deborah Campbell-Todd
© 1997 Grandreams Limited

Published by
Grandreams Limited
435-437 Edgware Road
Little Venice
London W2 1TH

Printed in Hong Kong

Long ago, God looked at the world he had created and at the people. He saw that they were wicked, and it made him sorry that he had made man.

Only one man found favour in God's eyes - a man named Noah. He had three sons, Ham, Shem and Japheth. This family was good and prayed to God every day.

God was sad and angry as he looked on the wicked world.

"I will blot out man and the beasts that crawl over the world," he said. "I am sorry I ever made them."

God said to Noah, "I have decided to destroy all that I have created. You must make an ark of gopher wood. It must have rooms on three decks, and a door in its side. Make a roof for it and cover it inside and out with pitch. Take yourself and all your family on board and two of every sort of animal, male and female, for I shall cause a great flood to cover the earth."

Noah did as God commanded and he and his family spent many days working on the boat.

Food was also gathered by Noah's family to feed themselves and the animals.

People came from miles around to watch and to laugh, but Noah carried on.

When the ark was finished, God told Noah to take his family on board, and then he sent the animals on to the ark, two by two.

"In seven days I shall send rain, and it will last for forty days and forty nights and every living thing I have created will be destroyed," God told Noah.

God then closed the door of the ark.

After seven days the rains began. The waters
began to rise, and the people outside the ark
realised that Noah had done the right thing.

The ark was soon lifted up on the water as
everything around it was washed away. The
rivers filled and the lakes overflowed - soon the
whole world was covered in water and God
destroyed every living thing except for those
safe on the ark.

The rains lasted for forty days and forty nights until even the highest mountain was covered by the water. Every living thing on earth was dead. God remembered Noah on his ark and sent a wind to dry up the water. The waters took 150 days to drop. The ark came to rest on the mountains of Ararat.

The waters continued to drop, and the
mountains could be seen. After forty days
Noah released a raven that flew about. Then
Noah released a dove. She could find nowhere
to perch and returned. Seven days later he
released her again and she returned with an
olive leaf. Seven days later the dove was
released and this time she did not return. Noah
knew the waters had all gone. He opened the
door of the ark.

The ground was dry.

"Take your family and leave the ark. Release the animals and let them go out over the earth. Begin a new life," God told Noah.

Noah built an altar and worshipped God, thanking him for saving them from the flood.

God blessed Noah and all his family, telling them to go out into the world and have many children. He also told them that he would never again send a flood to destroy the world.

God made a rainbow appear in the sky as a sign of his promise never to flood the earth again.